WOMEN OF THE BLUE RIDGE

SARAH LAMB

ISBN: 978-1-960418-00-5

Contents

Chapter		1
1.	Chapter 1	3
2.	Chapter 2	13
3.	Chapter 3	23
4.	Chapter 4	31
5.	Chapter 5	39
6.	Chapter 6	49
7.	Chapter 7	55
8.	Chapter 8	65
9.	Chapter 9	73
10.	Chapter 10	83
11.	Chapter 11	91

12. Epilogue   99

About the Author   104

For the real Frances...

Chapter 1

1940, Waynesboro, Virginia

Frances trudged up the stairs, pushing her dark hair from her eyes. It was good to be home. Even better that there was some daylight. Fishing around for the key in her purse, she found it and unlocked the door to the boarding house room.

The quiet strains of Tommy Dorsey and his Orchestra playing on the radio wafted out as she pushed the door open. Her sister Thelma looked up from a worn chair where she sat, feet soaking in a pan of Epsom salts and a book in her hand. "Good day?" she asked.

"Long," Frances sighed. "They are all long. I wish more people understood how hard we work in that factory. One day, I wouldn't say no to something more interesting, perhaps working in a nice store." She slipped off her shoes and set her purse down. Opening it, she dug around. "Payday though. I went to the bank."

Thelma smiled. "Makes it worth it," she said, easing her swollen feet out of the tub and drying them with a thin towel. "Want me to make you some water to soak in?"

Frances shook her head. "No, I'm fine. I was thinking about splurging a little," she said, dropping a few dollar bills into a tin. She carefully counted out the remainder of her money and dropped most of it into a glass jar. "There. That's rent and groceries. Minus the money for Mom and Dad, I've just enough left over to save toward that new blouse I wanted, and to treat us to a hamburger at the stand down the street."

With a laugh, Thelma asked, "Is it a hamburger you are wanting, or a look at that cute cook?"

"Both," Frances grinned, flipping her hair and going over to the small mirror hanging on the wall. She dabbed on a touch of lipstick. "I don't want to stay single forever! I'm twenty-two. Besides, it would be nice to have a guy to do things with on the weekends." She twisted the lipstick tube down and snapped the lid back on. "Coming with me?"

"Of course," Thelma said. "Who knows, I might just find a beau to catch my eye, too. Give me just a moment to get ready?"

Frances nodded, put her shoes back on her aching feet, and switched off the radio. She peeked through the window. Off in the distance, she could just make out the corner of the hamburger stand.

Did it really matter if she was hungry or just wanted to catch a glimpse of the cook? Both were valid reasons for treating herself on payday!

"Ready," Thelma said.

Walking down the stairs from their room, Frances glanced behind to make sure the door was shut and locked. She and Thelma had been there for a little over a year. She missed her family, but each time she got paid or a little extra money came their way, she and Thelma set it aside. They were going to buy their parents a home one day. That would help ease their financial worries.

Her mind drifted back to the tiny house they'd grown up in. Sometimes, when she thought about home, she could smell the sweet scent of ripe peaches. Their father was a tenant farmer who worked with peach trees, and that's how he made his living. He grew them, cared for them, and sold the saplings.

Their mother did whatever she could as well, washing and sewing to make a few coins, but it was never much. There in their small, Virginia rural area, everyone was as poor as they were. Being one of eleven made it a necessity to earn a living as you got older. Everyone needed to pitch in. The lack of jobs meant when the children grew up, they went to the larger towns or cities to find work, like she and Thelma had.

But for her, working meant there was the added goal of surprising her parents with a house. Buying their parents a house, a place to fully call their own without anyone to take it from them, was one of the things that kept her going. She'd eat nothing but bread for a week if she had to, but she'd never miss dropping a portion of her pay into that tin. Each time the tin grew full, she and Thelma went to the bank and deposited it. Right now, there wasn't a lot in the bank, but with hard work and consistency, it could grow. It already had.

They walked down the block and stopped at the corner. Their boarding house was in a good location, she reflected. A small corner store was nearby, the grocer was only about three blocks away, the bus picked up from a nearby corner and took them anywhere they wanted to go, and the hamburger stand was only a block away, if one of them wanted a quick bite.

Or a glance at the cute man flipping the burgers.

Frances smoothed her hair as they got closer, then tugged on her skirt.

"You look fine," Thelma said, not bothering to hide her smile.

Frances didn't answer, pretending not to hear her. They walked up to the stand. It wasn't too big. There was a counter with a dozen stools, three of them occupied. A tired looking teenage boy wiped the counter and looked up as they came closer.

"Menu?" he asked. His nametag said "Jimmy".

"We'll each take a hamburger," Frances said.

"Tomato? Lettuce? Mayo?" the boy asked.

"And pickles," Thelma said.

Jimmy nodded and leaned over to the window, where the white cap of the cook could be seen. "Cecil, two burgers with tomato, lettuce, mayo, and pickles."

Cecil looked up. He nodded, his eyes flicking toward Frances and Thelma, and he muttered something. Frances couldn't hear what he said, but a moment later, two Cokes were set before them.

"Oh, we didn't order those," Frances said.

"Compliments of the chef," the teenager said, winking. "He thinks you're cute."

Frances's cheeks colored and she ducked her head. Her eyes raised and met Cecil's through the window. She wanted to thank him, but her tongue felt tied. She felt that way every time they ate at the stand, or she walked past and saw him. He must live nearby, because sometimes they passed each other on the sidewalk. They didn't really say more than a hello, but that was enough for her.

Almost, anyway.

Thelma nudged her with her elbow. "Say something," she muttered.

"Thank you," Frances called. She wasn't sure if Cecil could hear, but he grinned at her and vanished. A few moments later, Jimmy was bringing them their hamburgers. They looked delicious. The buns were grilled, the lettuce crisp, and thick slices of bright red tomato peeked out.

Thelma lifted the top of her bun and nodded at the number of pickles. "If you're going to get us the star treatment, we should come here more often," her sister joked, unfolding her napkin and setting it in her lap.

"Maybe," Frances agreed, biting into her burger. It tasted just how she liked. Well done, steaming, and tasty. She frantically grabbed for a napkin as juices burst from the tomato. Dabbing her face, she looked around. Hopefully, Cecil hadn't seen anything running down her chin.

Cecil. Now that she knew his name, she wondered what else she could learn about him. Where did he live? What things did he like? Where else did he go when he wasn't working?

Another customer came and ordered, and Frances watched for a glimpse of the handsome cook as he accepted the order and a few minutes later set it on the order window.

"...if you want."

Frances looked over at her sister. Lost in her thoughts, she'd missed the entire thing Thelma said. "I'm sorry, can you say that again?" she asked.

With a grin to show exactly why she knew she had to repeat herself, Thelma said, "It's Friday and we both have off tomorrow. Want to stroll with me and window shop?"

"I'd love to," Frances answered. She couldn't linger much longer over her nearly finished burger.

"We can wander past here on the way home," Thelma said with a knowing smile.

Laughing, Frances finished her food, the last of the Coke, and stood. "Thanks again," she said to Jimmy, leaving a tip next to her plate. Her eyes sought for the cook, but he wasn't there. Disappointed, she turned, and she and Thelma spent the next hour looking at the window displays of the nearby shops. Other couples and entire families strolled along the main streets, pausing in front of the shop windows. It was a favorite pastime in their town on a fine evening. Window shopping never seemed to get old. Some of the shops tried to outdo each other with their outlandish displays. There was always something new and interesting to see.

"One day," Thelema said, pointing to a storefront, "I'm going to have a coat just like that. Perhaps in cream. Or blue." She tipped her head to the side as she considered.

"Mmm, I'll take that handbag," Frances said, motioning to one on a display. "Isn't the color perfect? I like the handle, too."

They turned, heading back toward the hamburger stand, and Frances couldn't help it. Her heart fluttered a little. Would Cecil be there? She was so busy trying to see inside the small order window she didn't realize Thelma had stopped. Looking over her shoulder, Frances paused to see what her sister was staring at.

There, leaning against the side of the hamburger stand stood Cecil. He had put on a button-up shirt over his white work t-shirt. His dark pants and shiny shoes showed the care he'd taken with getting dressed. Instead of the white cook's cap he'd been wearing earlier, his head was bare, with light brown hair neatly trimmed.

Cecil looked at her with a grin and asked, "Walk you home?"

Chapter 2

Frances felt her breath catch in excitement. He was asking to walk her home? For the first time, she wished it were a much longer walk than a block to their room. But she'd take what she could get. Maybe he'd walk slowly. She planned to.

"Sure," she said, raising her chin a bit. "I'd like that, thanks."

Thelma interjected, "I just remembered, I have to get something from the corner store. Go ahead, I'll see you back there."

Frances gave her sister a grateful look and a wave. Cecil stepped next to her. "Your friend?"

"Sister, actually," Frances said. "She's older than me by a little bit. We share a room."

He nodded. "Which way?"

"This way," Frances answered, and headed in the correct direction. They walked in silence for a moment. Nervously, she waited for him to say something. He didn't. Her mind stumbling over what to say, she blurted the first thing that came to mind. "Thanks again for the Coke."

He grinned at her. "Glad to do it."

He didn't say anything else, and she wondered if maybe he felt as shy as she did. "Have you been working there long?" she asked.

Cecil rubbed at his head. "A little while. Not too long, I guess. I'm lucky to have it. It can still be tough to get a job. I'd like to work at an automotive shop, but not too many people are driving right now, what with coming off the recession. Shoe leather's cheaper. They don't need me right now at any of the shops, but I'm hoping that changes."

He spoke in short sentences, which Frances found she liked. He wasn't one to waste words. To the point, as her father would say.

"Yes, I take all the hours I can get at the factory. It's hard work, and I'm sure they don't pay us enough for as much as we do, but I'm lucky to have the job." They paused as a woman pushing a baby carriage rolled in front of them.

Setting off again, slowly, they resumed their conversation.

"I help my folks with money," Cecil said. "I live by myself, but some gets given to them."

"I do the same," Frances said. "My dream is to make enough money to buy my parents a house. They deserve a nice place. It's not been easy for them. There were a bunch of us growing up, and my father wasn't able to get work sometimes."

Cecil nodded. "I understand. The Depression has hurt a lot of folks. At times, I wonder if we'll ever get to recover fully before something comes along and drags us back into another one."

That was a sobering thought. "I hope we do, and that it's a long time before that happens," Frances said. "It's ruined a lot of families, left a lot of people down and out."

"That's why you don't hear me complaining," he agreed. "Doesn't matter what it is. Even if it's not easy work, it's honest work. That's for me."

Frances smiled at him. She liked that. Judging by his arms, lean, but with calloused fingers, she could tell he didn't try to avoid work of any kind. Catching sight of her surroundings, she felt a little disappointed they'd almost arrived. Frances pointed to the boarding house. "That's me," she said.

"Are you kidding me?" Cecil shoved his hands in his pockets and let out a low whistle. He looked from the building to her. "You sure?"

"Of course I am," Frances answered, surprise filling her. What a strange question that was! "I should know where I live."

He laughed and pulled out a key from his pocket, holding it up. "Me too."

Her eyes widened. "Are you serious? We live in the same building?"

"I guess so," he said agreeably. "I wonder how I never noticed a pretty girl like you going in and out. No wonder we always passed on the sidewalk nearby."

Frances laughed. "I suppose it was for the same reason I never saw you going in and out. We work as much as we can to help our families."

They stood there a moment, staring at each other. "Well, see you later, I guess," Cecil said, opening the boarding house door and letting her go in first. They paused in the foyer.

"See you later," she agreed.

He didn't say anything more, so she went toward her room, looking over her shoulder once. He was still there, and gave her a little grin. Waving in return, she went around a corner and couldn't see him again.

Frances near floated back to her room and waited. It wasn't too long before Thema came back, an angry expression in her eyes.

"I cannot believe that woman," Thelma snapped, slamming the door behind her. She took off her hat and set it down on the small table they had, then yanked off her shoes before starting to pace as much as their tiny room allowed. "Do you know what that Mrs. Dixon said down at the general goods store?"

"What?" Frances asked.

Thelma took a deep inhale. "I had picked up a bar of scented soap. The kind that comes wrapped in that lavender paper with a tiny purple ribbon?" At her sister's nod of recognition, she continued. "I sniffed it, wondering what it smelled like. Mrs. Dixon comes around the corner and insinuated that I didn't have the money to buy it."

France's eyes flashed with anger. "I can't stand that woman."

"Me either," Thelma said. "I almost bought it out of spite, but I decided why should I? I stalked out and I won't be back. I'll do my shopping somewhere else. Every bit of it."

"As will I," Frances vowed. "That makes me angry. We work just as hard as anyone else. Harder maybe. Why do so many people look down on factory girls? After all, if it weren't for us, there are a lot of things that wouldn't be made as quickly as they are."

Thelma nodded grimly. "I agree. She won't get a penny of my money. It's not like it used to be, filthy and poor working conditions. It's hard work, yes, but it's honest work."

Frances blinked. Hadn't Cecil said almost the same thing just a short time ago? The thought made her smile. It made her happy he shared some of the same values she and her sister did.

Pacing back to the window, Thelma straightened herself to her full height and crossed her arms. "One day, you bet

I'm going to buy that soap. All the time. But I won't be buying it from her."

"Don't let her get you angry," Frances said. "She's probably just upset about something else. That doesn't give her a right to be rude to you, but don't take her words to heart."

Exalting loudly, Thelma nodded. "You are right." She went to the small cabinet where they kept their food, and filled a glass of water from a large bottle. "Now," she said, leaning against the cabinet. "Tell me, how was the walk home?"

Frances blushed. "It wasn't anything special," she said. "He's a little shy, I think. He didn't talk too much, but that's okay. He told me one day he'd like to be an auto mechanic."

"Always handy to know how to fix things," Thelma agreed.

"Mmm," Frances said, lost in thought. "I wonder when I'll get to see him again."

Her older sister's teasing smile shone across the room. "It's not even been an hour. Missing him again already?"

"Hardly," Frances said, tossing her hair. "But it was a short walk, and he is rather cute. I think I could like him."

"I need to meet a man, too," Thelma said. "Do you think he has an older brother?"

"I'll ask," Frances promised, "if I see him again and it comes up in the conversation."

Thelma clicked on the radio. A commercial for dish soap was playing.

"I didn't tell you," Frances said suddenly, interrupting the jingle that played. "Cecil lives here! In this building!"

Thelma looked surprised. "Is that so? Fancy never running into him before." A thoughtful look came over her face. "Who knows, little sister. Maybe the two of you were meant to be. Right place, right time. You looked good walking together down the street. Mama would have been pleased, I think."

"I'm not making plans to plant my roots just yet," Frances smiled. "Just a fella to see regular would be nice. But yes, who knows! I am looking forward to seeing him again. There's something about him, and I just can't explain it. But I really like him. I feel...comfortable around him. We are similar in some ways. Do you know he sends money home too?"

"Speaking of home," Thelma said, "it's your turn to write the letter this week."

"I will," Frances promised, going over to the small box of paper. "Anything you want me to tell Mama?"

"Yes," Thelma said. "Be sure to tell her all about Cecil."

"Oh you!" Frances said, and made a face.

Thelma laughed. "And tell her when we visit next, I can't wait for some peach cobbler. Send my love, too."

Frances nodded and set her head over the paper. Maybe she would mention Cecil. Or maybe she'd wait until they met again. There might be more to tell then. After a moment, she started writing. Mama looked forward to their letters, and she didn't want to disappoint her by not sharing as much as she could. She never talked about their hardships. In truth, their life was filled with more comfort than it had been at home. She and Thelma made enough for themselves, and some to set aside.

It didn't matter that their room was quite small. It held two beds, a small table, the worn chair, a small chest of drawers, and some hooks. That was more than enough for the two of them. If they wanted a change of scenery or to mingle a little, there was a parlor downstairs where the boarders could go. Meals were provided, at an additional fee, but Frances and Thelma usually only ate there for the evening meal. Their cabinet kept a modest cache of bread, crackers, butter, and jam, along with some apples. All enough to tide them over.

Frances nibbled on a piece of bread with jam as she pondered what to write about this time. Finally, in her neat handwriting, she wrote about the late spring flowers she'd observed, how she was looking forward to ripened tomatoes from the small potted plant they were growing on their windowsill, and asked about news of their siblings.

She'd set the pencil down and turned to get an envelope when there was a knock at the door. For some reason she couldn't explain, Frances's heart leapt into her throat.

Cecil?

Chapter 3

Frances's heart thumped and a sudden burst of butterflies filled her stomach. No one ever knocked on their door. *Was* it Cecil? She didn't know why she'd think that, but the hope was there. Smoothing her skirt as she rose, she hurried to the door and pulled it open. A woman stood there dressed in a pale pink dress with a white sweater. "I'm looking for Carla," she said. "I'm her new roommate?"

"Sorry, not sure who that is," Frances said, closing the door. Disappointment flooded her. Silly. *Why would it have been him?*

As she turned, she met Thelma's gaze. Her sister didn't say anything, just gave a little smirk. Frances rolled her eyes in return and put the letter into the envelope. "Do we have any stamps?" she asked.

"I'm not sure we do," Thelma said. "You might need to walk to the corner store."

"Alright," Frances said. "Want to join me?"

"You go ahead. I'm going to shampoo my hair while the washroom is free," Thelma answered.

"Sounds good," Frances said, pulling on her shoes.

"Who knows," Thelma teased, "you might run into Cecil..."

"Hush," Frances laughed, though she thought that wouldn't be a terrible thing. Not really.

Letter and purse in hand, she went downstairs and out of the building.

"Fancy seeing you again."

It was him. Cecil was standing next to another man about his age. Freezing, Frances lost her senses for a moment. With a smile, she turned. "Hello again."

"Heading out?" he asked.

"Yes, I needed a stamp. I'm going to the corner store."

"Well, okay. See you later." Cecil waved.

Slightly breathless, Frances gave her own wave and hurried down the sidewalk. She wondered if those were his eyes she felt on her, or if it was just her imagination. When she didn't see him on her return trip home, or the next day, Frances couldn't help but feel a little dejected. She peeked out her small window several times.

"Walk down and get a Coke at his stand if he's there," her sister suggested, looking up from her book. "You are going to drive us both crazy with your constant peering out the window."

Frances shook her head. "I'm not going to make up excuses to see him. And you know our rent goes up next month. I've got to mind my money."

"If you don't see him by next Friday, I say we go. I'll treat. I've some mad money," Thelma said. "I don't want to see you sitting around moping."

"I'm not moping," Frances argued.

"Pining then," her sister agreed.

"You are impossible," Frances laughed.

She couldn't help it though. Cecil *was* on her mind. It was strange, because she hadn't been trying to get a boyfriend, yet...he just stumbled into her life and now, she didn't want him to leave it.

Frances set herself near windows often that weekend, hoping to get a glimpse of him. She wondered if he was curious about her too. He must not have someone he was seeing, since he asked to walk her home. Making a point to linger more than usual in the downstairs sitting room, Frances kept one eye on the newspaper their landlady had a subscription to, and one eye on the front door. Still, she didn't see him.

Where was he? Frustration filled her.

When Monday came, as she left for work, she couldn't help but wonder if Cecil would be outside. Maybe she should have sat outside that weekend to catch a glimpse of him, not in the house. He didn't seem like the type who wanted to sit around indoors. Obviously, the hamburger stand wasn't open in the mornings, but maybe he would be outside right now, talking to someone or just enjoying the morning?

The bus came and she climbed on it, paying her fare. Just as it pulled out, she spotted him leaving the building. Drat that bus. If it had just been a moment or two late she could have said hello!

When the bus arrived at the factory, Frances pushed thoughts of anything but her job aside. Work was too difficult for Frances to let her mind wander. That's when accidents happened. With all the machines there, a person could lose a finger or have their sleeve get caught in a piece of equipment, potentially hurting them. Frances focused on her job and nothing else. She had to. The girls who didn't got injured, and injuries meant no income.

Her factory focused on making synthetic fabrics, in particular a type of rayon called acetate. They were one of the first to make colored-sealed acetate yarn. This yarn was used to make clothes and was incredibly high in demand. As a result, the factory was quite large. The building was also newer. It had been built on that particular site because there was a river nearby, and it provided many jobs for the community. Coming out of the Depression, it was a blessing for many. It sure was for Frances and Thelma.

The factory improved the town by upgrading a school, roads, sidewalks, sewer systems and more. They'd spent over a half million in the community, an almost unheard of amount in this small town. While Frances didn't work in the part of the factory that did the chemical treatments, the small fibers flying around irritated her lungs at times, and the smell of the processing chemicals always seemed to fill the air.

Though she was used to it, each day as she left, she couldn't stop herself from gulping in fresh breaths of clean, untainted air. As grateful for the job as she was, Frances couldn't see herself working there forever. One day, she'd love to work in a large department store. That was her dream job, and perhaps something that she'd do well at. How fun it would be, being surrounded by goods for the home or clothing, and helping customers find just the right thing. Still, she'd never complain about having a job. There were many who didn't.

Thursday came, and an exhausted Frances made her way home on the bus. Her feet ached, and so did her head. The constant din of the machinery usually faded into the background, but today it didn't, instead causing a harmonic that resonated in a painful way.

Slowly, she walked along the sidewalk to the boarding house. Maybe she'd see Cecil today. She hoped so. Not that she minded going to the hamburger stand again, but she didn't want anyone to think that she was being too forward. She and Thelma had to be careful. As single women, all it would take was a rumor to get them thrown out of their boarding house. She couldn't risk that. It would make it much more difficult to keep her job.

With a yawn, Frances went up the front walkway, eager to get inside and soak her feet and rest. As she put her hand on the doorknob, it suddenly shifted, and the door opened, sending her tumbling forward, and into the arms of someone.

Chapter 4

Frances threw her arms out to catch herself, and found them up against a warm, lean, chest. Surprised, she looked up and into the eyes of Cecil. Trying to regain her balance, she clung to him, then felt his strong, steadying arms around her as she was righted.

"Trying to knock me off my feet?" he grinned.

She laughed and teased, "Are you sure it wasn't the other way around?"

His loud guffaw made her laugh again. "I'm terribly sorry," Frances said. "I guess we had quite the timing, huh?"

"You said it," he said, stepping to the side to let her in. "You get hurt?"

"No," she shook her head. "I'm fine. I hope I didn't step on your feet though."

"Even if you had, I wouldn't have felt it," he shrugged. "You look light as a feather." He eyed her critically. "You eat enough?"

Before she could answer, he said, "Come by the stand tonight. It's half price burgers."

"Do you work there tonight?" Frances asked.

"Yep." He hooked his thumbs into his waistband and tugged. "Tonight and tomorrow."

"I'll see what Thelma has planned," Frances said. "You make a fine burger. That might taste good tonight."

Cecil looked down at his feet, then back up at her. "If you come by around seven, I leave at eight. Could walk you home if your sister needs to go shopping again."

Frances's stomach tingled with excitement. "That sounds nice," she said. All of a sudden she felt nervous. Did she look as awkward as she felt?

He nodded. "Okay. See you later." He left, closing the door behind him. Frances shook her head. Cecil asked her to come by...and offered to walk her back. Did that mean he liked her?

As she puzzled this, she went into her room, realizing the headache was gone. Thelma was there, eating an apple and doing a puzzle from the newspaper.

"Guess what?" Frances asked.

"You saw Cecil?" her sister grinned.

"How could you tell?" Frances asked, surprised.

"Because you are glowing," Thelma laughed. "I'm still up for buying a Coke tomorrow though."

"He told me it's half-priced hamburgers tonight. Want to go?"

"Sure," Thelma said. "He say anything else?"

"Cecil sure isn't much of a talker," Frances said. "Everything he says is quick, to the point. But he did say if we got there around seven, he left at eight, and if you had to do some shopping afterward, he could walk me home." She looked at her sister expectantly.

"Alright," Thelma said. "I sure am not going to Mrs. Dixon's store, but I can take a long walk by myself, so you two can go together."

Frances beamed. "You're the best sister. Thank you."

"Not too long though," Thelma warned. "My feet are hurting, and I have to get up for the early shift tomorrow, you know."

Nodding, Frances went into her dresser drawer, opened a small box, and put some money into her purse. "That's why I'm buying dinner!"

"Say," Thelma said, "Do you think if you two get married, we get free hamburgers?"

Frances laughed and didn't answer. What a preposterous idea! Marriage? They hardly knew each other. But... the question turned itself over and over in her mind and she found herself taking a moment to really consider the question. If she were to get married to Cecil, what would it be like?

An hour later, she twirled in front of her sister, as best as their tiny room could allow. "How do I look?" Frances asked.

"Perfect," Thelma said.

Frances was pleased with the answer. She was wearing her second-best blouse with light blue pinstripes on it, a dark blue skirt, and her low heels. Putting on a dab of lipstick, she nodded in satisfaction. "I'm ready. Are you?"

Thelma nodded. "All ready," she said.

The walk to the stand wasn't a long one, but Frances had to keep herself from going too fast. It wouldn't do to get there and be hot and sweaty. Plus, her feet hurt too. It was time to look for some better, more comfortable shoes. Why didn't they make such a thing for women? You never heard men complaining about their feet. That was proof their shoes were made more comfortably.

"Word got around, I guess," Thelma said. "It's packed!"

Thelma was right. Each stool was occupied, and several people were standing around or sitting on the grass holding plates. As usual, there were quite a few young men in uniforms from Fishburne Military Academy gathered. It was a favorite spot for many of them to gather.

"I guess we could wait a moment?" Frances said. "Someone's sure to finish soon."

Her sister nodded, and luckily, it wasn't but a moment later two people did get up. Frances and Thelma hurried for the stools and sat. It was the same teenager taking orders as the week before. He nodded at them. "Be with you shortly."

"Take your time," Frances said, as she settled on the stool. Raising herself up a bit, she strained to see through the small window to catch a glimpse of Cecil. There he was, his back turned to her, as he cooked several hamburgers at once.

"Take your order?" Jimmy asked.

"Two burgers," Thelma said, "and two Cokes."

"I remember you," Jimmy grinned. "Made same as before?"

Frances nodded. "Yes, thank you. You look pretty tired," she said.

"I am," he agreed. "Had school all day, now this, but it helps the family, you know?" He turned and filled the glasses, setting them down a moment later. A customer held up a hand and the teenager hurried over.

"I don't know of anyone who isn't trying to help their family," Thelma sighed. "It makes you wonder how long it will take us to recover from the effects of the Depression."

Frances nodded, taking a sip of her drink. "Yes. I know. What's good though, is we all learned how we are made of sterner stuff. We got very creative using what we did have, and still managed to have good times."

"Hey!" Cecil's head popped up through the window and he waved to her.

Frances waved back. "Hey yourself!"

The burgers were ready soon after. They ate, and then Thelma winked. "I'll see you back home," she said, as Cecil took off his apron and waited a short distance away.

Walking over to him, Frances felt a little shy. "Good burgers again," she said.

"As many as I make each day, I'm pretty much an expert," he said. "Could make 'em with my eyes shut. Walk you home?"

Frances nodded, and fell into step with him.

"How'd your day go?" he asked.

"Pretty well. My job is pretty much the same each day."

"You work at Dupont?" Cecil asked.

"Yes. How did you know?" Frances said.

He shrugged. "It's the biggest factory around. A lot of women work there. You like it?"

That made her pause. Finally, she answered, "It's a job. It's hard, but I'm grateful to have it. The people I work with are good, and the bus drops off close, so I'm happy about that. Right now, I've got weekends off, too."

"That's always nice," he agreed.

The boarding house appeared, just as last time—too soon for Frances's liking.

"Well, here we are." He opened the front door for her. "I've got off Sunday," he said. "You?"

She nodded. Was he going to ask her out?

Cecil dug his toe into the scuffed wood floor in the foyer, and his eyes followed it. "Want to have dinner with me and my folks?" he asked. "I go every Sunday, and might have mentioned walking you home. Now my folks want to see what you look like."

Frances smiled. "I'd like that," she agreed. "As long as it's not trouble."

"Oh no," he said. "I'd like that fine. I'll meet you at the front of the building at four in the afternoon Sunday. I'll drive us. Got myself a truck yesterday. Just to warn you though, my mother isn't going to like you." He waved and disappeared, leaving Frances staring at his back in shock.

Chapter 5

"Just like that! He said it and then walked off!" Frances said, throwing her hands up in the air. "What does that even mean? Why in the world did he say that and leave?"

Thelma shook her head. "That's a man for you. Never giving enough context. Are you still going to go?"

"I guess so. I want to see why his mother won't like me." Frances bit her lip.

"It could be something as simple as he's her baby and not good enough for anyone," Thelma suggested. "Or it could be she had a preconceived notion of who he would marry already."

"You mean, like someone with some pedigree and wealth? Not the daughter of a tenant farmer who sells peach trees?" Frances raised an eyebrow, then dropped into a chair. "Some people."

"We won't put her in the class with Mrs. Dixon just yet," Thelma said. She pursed her lips in thought. "You wear my yellow sweater, and that navy skirt of yours with a white blouse. That would look nice."

"I will," Frances said, straightening. "I'll show them I'm good enough for anybody."

"That's my girl," Thelma approved. "Now, I'm going to bed. I've the early shift."

Frances nodded, and picked up the mystery book she'd borrowed from the library and moved closer to the small lamp. They were lucky to live in a town with a place to borrow books. Why, their library had been only the third in the state to open, using tax dollars. After a time, she started to yawn, marked her page, and went to bed herself.

Try as she might, she couldn't help but wonder what offense she'd committed already, to be looked down on by Cecil's mother. She hadn't even met the woman! It took so long for her mind to calm down, morning came well before she was ready. Getting herself together, Frances made it to the bus stop just in time, and clocked in at the factory.

It was hard to keep her mind on her work that day, and twice she'd had a near miss with a piece of equipment. It wasn't until the second time she'd almost had a serious accident that Frances firmly pushed all thoughts but work out of her mind and, thankfully, finished the shift uneventfully.

On the way home, she watched as off in the distance, the Blue Ridge Mountains rose. She enjoyed the scenery. The various shades of blue contrasted wonderfully with each other. In the fall, the leaves turned the most incredible scarlet, burnt orange, yellow, and rust. Mother Nature outdid herself when she created this area. It was peaceful, beautiful, and filled with history. It made her feel proud to be living here in such a place.

The bus stopped and a man climbed on, choosing to sit in front of her on the next aisle. He shook out his newspaper, and the headline caught her eye.

Escalating Conflict Between China and Japan!

Frances gave a small frown. If things continued the way they had been, it was possible the United States might get involved. If men were called into a draft, could their economy recover from the already strained situation it was in? She was shaken from the thought as the bus stopped again. Now, new thoughts rushed in as she saw the front of the boarding house, where she was to meet Cecil in two days.

Would his mother really not like her?

***

Frances waited nervously in front of the boarding house. It was four in the afternoon, but Cecil wasn't there yet. Suddenly, a truck riddled with bullet holes pulled up along the curb and honked the horn. Cecil's grinning face was leaned over to look at her through the rolled down passenger window.

"Hey!" he shouted.

"Is this yours?" Frances asked, torn between amazement he owned a vehicle, and shock that it was covered in bullet holes.

"Sure is," he said, coming around and holding her door. "Got a great deal on it. Used to belong to a bootlegger."

"I...see. Is that why there are bullet holes in it?"

"Yep! He got them trying to get away." Cecil shut her door and climbed into the driver's seat proudly.

"Well, that's an interesting story," she said. *Thelma might never believe this.* "Did he...make it away?"

"I'm not sure," Cecil admitted. "Maybe that's why I have it now."

Frances gulped and nodded. How in the world did you answer something like that?

"It's not too bad a drive," he told her. "About an hour. Just relax. Aren't the seats terrific?"

"Yes, they are. And that sounds fine," Frances answered.

"This thing is specially modified," Cecil went on. "Did you know bootleggers have all kinds of special things on their vehicles? There are secret compartments in here. Handy to stash things. I fixed the brakes though," he said, turning onto a twisty road.

"The...the brakes?"

"Yep. They were modified too. You know, one higher than the other. Makes for hairpin turns. I set em back to the normal way. Left the kill switch on, though. Might come in handy. You never know."

Frances blinked. "I see," she said.

"Don't worry, I won't use it," he assured her. "But if there was ever a reason to, one hit of this switch and all the lights go out."

She could tell how proud he was of the car. "It runs real nice," she offered.

Cecil grinned. "Sure does," he agreed. "Check out this speed!" He pressed down on the accelerator and sped up.

They approached a tight turn. Frances grabbed onto the door, sure her face was a little green. As they took the curve, a large truck came the opposite way and honked at them. Her heart was hammering in terror as they whizzed past the blaring horn, only inches to spare.

Cecil looked over at her. "I'll take it easy," he said. "Just wanted to show you all the power in her. Isn't it great?"

"Won...wonderful," Frances gulped. As he slowed, she finally relaxed into the seat, then leaned forward and looked over at him. "I want to ask you something. You've had me a little worried, ever since you mentioned your mother might not like me."

"Oh, no might about it," Cecil said. "She won't like you." His frank manner startled her, but he shot a quick look at her and said, "Doesn't matter though. It's not her you are going out with."

Frances opened her mouth to answer, then closed it. *Going out with? Were they dating then? She sure didn't recall agreeing to that.*

He continued, as though he hadn't ever paused. "My mother just gets worried, that's all. Times are tough. If I find a girl to marry, I need the money I've been giving them to take care of the family I'll be making. Plus, I'm the oldest. She'd not gone through this before. You know how it is. Parents don't want to lose their children to someone else."

"That makes sense," Frances agreed. His words made her feel better. But also meant no older brother for Thelma. "I'll keep that in mind, and try not to get offended."

"I think it'll just be us this evening," he added. "My little brothers aren't in town this weekend."

Frances nodded, then realized he might be able to see her motion. "I look forward to meeting your parents," she said. "I'm sure we'll have a good evening, even if it's just us four."

Cecil shrugged, and didn't say too much until they pulled up in front of a modest home. It was tidy outside with some bright-colored flowers planted by neatly trimmed bushes. He opened the door and helped Frances out of the car. The home's front door opened and a woman with graying hair rushed out.

"Welcome home," she said, taking Cecil into an embrace. "My boy. How are you? Eating enough?"

"Yes, Mother," he said, returning her hug and pulling back. He moved near Frances. "This is Frances."

"A pleasure to meet you," Frances said, holding out her hand. "Thank you for inviting me."

The hand that was given to her was as limp as a fish, and Cecil's mother didn't say anything. Instead, she turned and walked back to the house. Frances gave Cecil a worried look, but he just smiled reassuringly. She followed him inside, to a small but cozy house, the smell of dinner filling it.

Cecil greeted a man in a chair, who stood at seeing them. "Frances, this is my dad. Robert Hall."

"Mr. Hall," she said politely. "It's nice to meet you."

Mr. Hall nodded, shook her hand, and pointed to the sofa. "Sit," he said. "Relax."

"Perhaps I should see if your mother needs help?" Frances asked.

"I don't," came the reply as Mrs. Hall stepped into the room. "Are you insinuating that I can't cook?" She wore a hurt expression on her face as she held a worn dishcloth.

"No, ma'am," Frances said, wishing she could sink into the brown sofa and disappear. "I just wanted to be polite. My mother would skin me alive if I didn't offer."

The look on the other woman's face softened, but only a little. She nodded with a humph. "It'll be ready in a little," she said and disappeared again.

Frances took a breath in and tried not to look as uncomfortable as she felt. Cecil hadn't been kidding. She wasn't sure how she was going to make it through dinner.

Chapter 6

"So, tell us about yourself," Mr. Hall said, spooning peas on top of his mashed potatoes. He passed the bowl to his wife.

"I'm one of eleven children," Frances started. "About in the middle. My older sister and I board together, and work at the same factory, though different shifts."

"Factory?" Mrs. Hall sniffed, as she held the bread basket toward Frances.

Her eyes lowered, Frances took a piece of bread. "Thank you," she murmured.

"Eleven, huh?" Mr. Hall said over his glasses. "Hard to raise that many. Especially nowadays."

"Yes," Frances agreed. "That's why as soon as possible, we've left to work and send home money to help our family and the younger ones still at home."

Mrs. Hall looked adoringly at Cecil. "Our boy does the same. He makes it so much easier on us. Of course," she said, looking back at Frances, "we didn't have more children than we could take care of. He does this simply to show his love. Not because we can't provide for our children."

Frances was grateful for the bite of dry chicken in her mouth. It gave her a moment to think of a reply. Luckily, she didn't have to.

Mr. Hall broke in, "Enough of that. Cecil, my boy, I hear they're going to require young men to be chosen for a peacetime draft. It's just waiting for the president to sign off on it."

Cecil nodded. "I heard that too. If it will pass, I don't know. If it does, I won't shirk. I'll do my duty to serve and protect, just like those who came before me have done."

His father nodded approvingly.

Mrs. Hall said, twisting her napkin, "I hope it doesn't come to that. I don't want my boys sent to war."

Frances sat quietly as the three spoke. She wondered if she should add to the conversation, or if it would make Mrs. Hall's jabs at her worse. She didn't have to wonder for long.

Mrs. Hall asked, "I suppose you have a lot of brothers who will be up for the draft?" At Frances's nod, she continued, "What does your father do? Does he need them to help with his business?"

Quietly, Frances answered, "No, he doesn't. My father is a tenant farmer. He sells peach trees. My mother takes in laundry." Raising her head, almost defiantly, she said, "It's not easy work, and it's not glamorous, high paying work, but people like them are the backbone of our country. They do hard, thankless work so that their children, and their children's children, have an advantage they didn't have."

Mr. Hall harrumphed, while Mrs. Hall shook her head. "A shame people have to live that way."

Her jaw clenched, Frances forced herself not to stab each bite of the meal with her fork, as angry as she felt. When dinner was over, she was incredibly grateful. Reaching deep to summon her politeness, she asked, "May I help with your dishes, Mrs. Hall?"

The other woman looked at her. "No, I'll manage, thank you. I'm sure you wouldn't break any, but you understand. Also, it's not polite to have a guest wash dishes."

Frances wasn't sure if that was a backhanded compliment, that she was a guest and wouldn't break the dishes, or if it was another well-hidden insult. With a nod, she smiled and said, "Thank you for the wonderful meal. It was very kind of you to invite me."

Wonderful wasn't the word she wanted to use. She wanted to say tasteless, dry, and with offending conversation, but instead, she smiled neutrally.

"We better go," Cecil said. He stood up and moved toward the front door. Frances followed, gratefully. "Work tomorrow," he said. "Long drive."

Goodnights were exchanged, and when she climbed back into the truck, Frances leaned her head back and sighed. Cecil slid in and looked over at her. "You survived," he said.

"Barely. I'd really hoped you were exaggerating your mother's reaction to me," she said.

Cecil put the truck in gear and pulled out. "Nope. She's that way with almost everyone. That's just her. Never mind her."

"That's a little hard to do," Frances said. She looked out the window.

Neither of them said much on the drive home. It had gotten dark, and in the deep shadows of the car, she was sure he couldn't see her trying to hold back tears. Frances was grateful when they pulled up to the boarding house. Cecil let her out at the curb. With a wave, Frances called, "Thanks again. I'll see you around," and hurried inside.

Thelma was waiting, and Frances met her sister's eyes, her own filled with disappointment. "That bad?" Thelma asked.

"It was horrible. If she wasn't insulting me, she was making a snide comment about me. I've never been so grateful to be home."

"I'm sorry," Thelma said. She was quiet a moment, and then asked the question Frances had been asking herself the whole drive home. "Are you two going out again?"

"No way," Frances said. "When you marry someone, you also marry their family. I don't want her for my mother-in-law. I like him, but you know, we don't really know each other too well. There are plenty of cute fellows out there. I'll find one if I look hard enough. However, after tonight's experience, I'm not interested at all."

With a nod, Thelma squeezed Frances's hand. "I understand. Are you going to tell him that though?"

Cecil's comment about going out with her sprang to mind. He seemed to be quite serious about them. Frances was quiet for a long moment. "I guess I have to, don't I?"

Chapter 7

Frances felt fortunate. Almost an entire week had gone by and she hadn't run into Cecil. As she walked home from the store, she was so lost in thought she didn't notice him calling to her from across the street.

"Hey! Hallo!"

She shouldn't have even thought his name. Now, she'd jinxed herself.

Frances raised her head, gave a tight smile and nod, but continued on her way. Footsteps pounded behind her, and she cringed, knowing that he was likely following her.

He was.

"Wait up. How are you?" Cecil asked, taking her shopping bag.

"I'm fine, thanks. But I can carry my own bag." She tried to get it back, but he shook his head.

"Nah, not while I'm here. You avoiding me?" he joked. "It's been a whole week almost, and this is the first I've seen you."

"Yes, I've been busy," Frances said. She walked a little quicker. The sooner she got home, perhaps the sooner this conversation would be over.

"You aren't still sore about Sunday dinner, are you? And my mother?"

Frances stopped. She yanked her bag out of Cecil's arms and answered, "Not at all. I've simply decided that I'm not interested in getting involved with anyone—or their family—at this time."

"What do you mean?" he asked, surprised. He reached over and grabbed at her bag, pulling on it.

"Will you stop? I'm perfectly capable of carrying my own bag," Frances said, turning away and hugging the bag.

"Why won't you let me help you?" Cecil asked, grabbing it harder and tugging.

"You are making a scene," Frances hissed. "Give me my groceries."

"Fine," Cecil growled.

He let go, just as Frances gave one final tug. There was a loud ripping sound, and Frances gave a small shriek. The grocery bag ripped. Now, lying on the sidewalk was a broken jar of pickles, a few wrapped packages of bread and cheese soaking up the pickle juice, but worst of all, a split bag of flour that had burst all over her.

As Frances looked down at her favorite skirt covered in flour, her shoes now with white splotches, and the damaged groceries, she let out a frustrated scream.

"Cecil Hall, I never want to see you or your horrible mother ever again," Frances burst out, scooping what was left of her groceries into her arms and running off, sobbing.

She ran into the boarding house, not caring that she looked a mess. Thelma looked up at her entry and gasped. "What happened?"

"That awful Cecil Hall. He kept grabbing at my groceries and look what happened! The pickles broke and are laying on the sidewalk. The flour burst all over me, and I'm sure the bread and the cheese are ruined." She sniffled, and wiped her eyes with the clean handkerchief Thelma handed her.

"You poor dear," her sister clucked. "Go get cleaned up. Let me have your outfit. I bet I can brush most of that out."

Nodding, Frances left the bundles to go change.

"Bread and cheese are fine," Thelma said a moment later as Frances appeared again. "That's lucky."

"I'm so mad, I never want to see him again," Frances said, furiously shaking her flour-covered clothes over the wastebasket.

"I'll work on your blouse. I bet we can have it righted soon," Thelma assured her.

"I just can't believe he did this," Frances fumed.

"Maybe he was just trying to be helpful," Thelma said, frowning as she brushed at a spot on the flour-covered blouse. "Men are like that. They want to help, but sometimes they just aren't very good at it."

Frances stopped shaking her skirt, a thoughtful expression on her face. Then it hardened, and she resumed shaking her skirt out vigorously. Little white puffs flew about the room. "Maybe. But I told him to leave me alone, and I meant it."

Thelma looked at her sideways. Carefully, she asked, "I know dinner didn't go so well the other night. But I wonder, are you mad at Cecil, or at his mother?"

"Both," Frances answered. "And I don't want to talk about it anymore."

"Alright," Thelma agreed. "But just so you know, it's okay to like one and not the other."

Neither spoke further. Her skirt was almost normal looking when there was a knock at the door.

"I wonder who that is," Thelma said. Frances shrugged and wiped her shoes with a damp rag to remove the flour.

Thelma handed her the now cleaned blouse, went to the door and opened it, then crossed her arms, leaning against the frame. "What do you want?" she asked.

Frances looked up. Cecil stood, a brown grocery bag in his arms and a sad expression on his face.

"I just wanted to apologize. I don't know what all else Frances bought, but I replaced your flour and your pickles."

"Mm." Thelma gave him a stern look.

Cecil handed over the bag, and shoved his hands into his pocket. "Forgive me? I just wanted to help."

Frances didn't answer.

"Want to get an ice cream?" he asked her. "We could take my truck. I'm working on patching up the bullet holes."

Thelma's head jerked up. "Bullet holes?" she gasped.

"Yeah. It used to belong to a bootlegger, but it's mine now," Cecil couldn't keep the pride out of his voice. "Once it's patched and repainted, no one will ever know."

"Bullet holes," Thelma repeated. She sagged slightly.

"Just a few," he assured her. "Not more than a dozen."

Frances couldn't help it. A small giggle escaped. Thelma's face made her laugh. The expressions on people's faces when they saw them driving along were amusing.

"So, is that a yes?" Cecil asked.

She shrugged. "I guess."

His face lit up. "Met you at the curb," he said, and left.

Thelma carried in the grocery bag and peered in. "A large jar of pickles and a large bag of flour. I guess he is sorry. But you didn't tell me about the truck! I'm not sure that's safe for you to ride around in. You know how modified those cars are. Made for speed and quick getaways." Her eyes narrowed. "You aren't going around speeding and acting dangerous in that thing, are you?"

Frances fluffed her hair and turned. "In all the mess with his mother, I guess I forgot to tell you about it. It's safe though, I promise. He changed a lot on it to make it more like a normal vehicle, and when I asked him to, he slowed down."

"Mmhmm. I thought you didn't want to see him again? Well, you'd better either set him straight or end things before we have any more damaged groceries and you get a reputation as a girl who plays around," Thelma warned.

"I will," Frances said. "I'm going to see what he says. Then I'll decide. I'm not going to play around. Who has time for that? For sure, not me!"

Just as she stepped to the front of the boarding house, Cecil pulled up to the curb. She climbed in, and they drove a few blocks to the ice cream stand. After ordering, vanilla for her, chocolate for him, they sat at one of the small tables, enjoying the bowls of ice cream and the sunshine.

Frances didn't say anything. She wanted to, but she wasn't sure what to say. She was still hurt by his mother's comments.

"Look," Cecil said, finally. "I meant what I said the other night. Don't let my mother get under your skin. Like I said on the way there, she's not the one going out with you."

Swallowing hard, Frances asked, "Does that mean you want us to go out?"

"If you'll have me," he said, scraping his spoon against the bowl. "Maybe see where it goes. No pressure."

Frances stared at him for a long moment. There were a lot of thoughts in her mind. His mother had been hurtful, but Cecil wasn't. He didn't treat her any less for working in a factory, living in a single room with her sister, or for being the daughter of hardworking, but poor parents. Perhaps his parents just needed a little time to see the same things Cecil did.

But then she shook her head. It still didn't excuse the unkind things her mother said. "I don't know if I can handle the way your mother treated me," she said softly. "It really hurt my feelings. I didn't do anything to deserve the way she spoke to me."

Cecil nodded, his gaze in the distance. "No, you didn't," he agreed after a moment. "My folks...well, you know how it is. There's only so much you can say to them."

Her shoulders tense, Frances dragged her spoon through the vanilla ice cream, making a little tunnel.

"I'm going to talk to her," he promised. "That is, if you think you'll go out with me again." He fixed his eyes on hers.

Was that worry in them? Hope? She wasn't sure. Regardless, she knew that Cecil would keep his word. Whether or not it made a difference in how his mother treated her, she wasn't sure.

Thelma's words came back to her, that she could like one and not the other. It was true. She could.

"I'd like that," Frances said quietly, looking into her ice cream before looking up at him. She took a deep breath. "Let's see where it goes. No pressure. I'm just sorry your mother doesn't care for me." She looked through her lashes at him almost shyly. "I hope that doesn't make things difficult for you."

"Doesn't matter," Cecil said. "Where you go, I go."

Quiet for a long moment, Frances let the words wash over her and fill her with a warmth she didn't know she needed until that very moment. Though Cecil had said them in his usual quick and offhand tone, she knew it meant much more than a surface comment. She could tell by the way he snuck glances at her.

Frances leaned her head back and looked up at the sky. She felt like changing the subject, but what burst out of her mouth wasn't planned. "Do you think they'll call up the draft?"

"I do," Cecil said, crumpling a paper napkin. "Things have gotten real bad. But America always pulls through. We've done it before, we'll do it again, if needed." He looked over at her. "You women have done more than your fair share to help, too. If there's a war, I imagine like before, factories will be converted or increase production of needed goods."

Frances nodded. "I suspect you will be right."

"If..." Cecil cleared his throat. "If it were to happen, me getting called up, think you'd write me?"

"Of course," Frances said. She reached over shyly and touched his arm before pulling her hand back. "I'd write you each day."

Cecil searched her eyes for a moment. He looked about to say something when a man sat down at the table next to him and opened his paper. Both Frances and Cecil looked over at him and his paper, a reflex habit.

However, Frances wished she hadn't looked. The large headline made Frances close her eyes for a moment as the words no one wanted to see were printed, in oversized letters.

Draft Bill Signed By President.

Chapter 8

Over the next two weeks, a somber tone seemed to have settled over the United States, and in Waynesboro, Virginia, it was no different. It seemed that everything in the newspaper was about the impending war, for it wasn't doubted by anyone that the United States would be called into it.

One-by-one, young men from the young age of eighteen to men up to age sixty-five, with established families and jobs, perhaps even grandchildren, were required to sign up for the peacetime draft. Friends and family gathered, but when they parted, none of them said 'when we next get together,' but instead 'if I don't come back, then I want you to remember...'.

England had already started food rationing, and it was likely that the United States would follow at some point, as supplies were being gathered for the possibility of war. Advertisements for defense bonds seemed plastered everywhere.

Though plans were being made both to go to war if need be, and what would happen if someone didn't return, throughout it all, the citizens remained calm. Life still went on. Schools were open, movies were watched, in fact, Walt Disney had been working very hard on an animated film many people were excited about, *Fantasia*. Marketed as something both the young and the old would enjoy, everyone was curious, as anything he'd made was quite a treat to watch. Set to debut November 13, 1940 on Broadway, it was hoped it would soon make its way to Virginia.

Thelma looked up from the letter she was writing to their parents. "Any news to share?" she asked.

"Only give my love," Frances replied. "There's not much else right now."

It was true. Life was work, a weekly outing with Cecil on Saturday or Sunday afternoons, and a weekly visit to the hamburger stand for a burger and Coke, usually on

Fridays, so Cecil could walk her home. When together, they tried not to talk about the thing everyone was most worried about.

Which, and when, young men would be called up, Cecil included.

Thelma nodded, wrote a little more, and then folded the letter. "It's nice out," she said. "I'm going to walk this to the post box. Want to join me?"

"I do," Frances said. "I'd like to get a little yarn. I'm going to knit Cecil a new scarf along with some socks. I think it's going to be a cold winter. It's already getting brisk."

Shrugging her coat on, Thelma made a sound of agreement. Frances found hers, and her purse, and followed Thelma out of the building. The sky was darkening early, threatening rain.

"Oh dear, we had better hurry," Frances said.

"I couldn't see that from the window," Thelma agreed. "If we move fast enough, we might beat it."

They walked quickly, and had just made it to the store when the first drops of rain fell. Thelma purchased a stamp while Frances quickly made her yarn selection. Though she'd hurried, by the time she'd paid, a fierce storm was raging. Rain was pouring, while the wind was blowing.

"My goodness," Thelma gasped from the shop's doorway. "Should we stay and wait it out?"

"We'll miss dinner if we do," Frances said.

"Do you remember the menu?" Thelma asked, watching a man's hat blow off and skip down the street.

"Chicken and dumplings," Frances answered.

"We go," Thelma said, pulling her jacket tightly. "Ready?"

They headed into the storm. Frances and Thelma walked as quickly as they could. The wind whipped, tearing at their coats, while rain pelted them, at times blinding their vision. Frances stepped into a puddle and groaned. She'd never get her shoes dry for tomorrow. They were still three blocks away.

A vehicle pulled alongside them and honked. "Get in!" a familiar voice shouted.

It was Cecil!

Gladly, Frances and Thelma climbed into the truck.

"I'm so sorry," Frances said, "we are getting the inside soaked."

"Don't mind a bit," Cecil said. "Not every day I get to save two pretty damsels in distress. Heading home?"

"Yes," Thelma said, dabbing at her face with her handkerchief. "Thanks for that. It's appreciated."

"I'll get you as close to the curb as I can," Cecil said. "Boy, look at this storm. We closed early today. The stand was shaking something fierce. I don't usually drive to work, but glad I did today."

"Can we save you a spot at dinner?" Frances asked. "Chicken and dumplings tonight."

"Sounds good," he agreed, pulling alongside the curb. "See you in a few."

Frances and Thelma climbed out of the car, racing to the front door. "That boyfriend of yours has great timing," Thelma said. "Here. Give me your coat and yarn. I'll take it to the room. You go grab some chairs."

With a nod, Frances handed the requested items and went into the dining room. The table was half full, but she didn't have a hard time getting three spots next to each other. Thelma and Cecil arrived at the same time and sat.

"If you hadn't come for us, we'd have been in terrible condition," Frances said, looking up at Cecil. "Thank you again."

Cecil's ears were turning pink. How had she never noticed they did that when he was embarrassed?

"It wasn't anything," he answered, taking a roll and passing along the basket. "How'd you two get trapped in the storm?"

"Thelma was posting a letter," Frances said. "I went with her to buy something."

"It wasn't raining when we left here," Thelma said. "I guess we just had some rotten timing."

Cecil shook his head. "Nope. Was perfect for me."

Frances laughed. "My hero."

"Take care of yourself next time," Cecil warned. "I don't want anything to happen to you."

"Oh, I'm fine," Frances smiled. "But thank you."

"I mean it," Cecil said. He set down his fork and met her eyes. "I wouldn't know what to do without you. I don't want to ever be without you." His expression was serious as he searched her face. "Promise me."

Frances's chest tightened. It felt hard to breathe. "I...I promise," she whispered.

She blinked a few times, trying to get her mind to work. Beside her, Cecil had picked his fork back up. On her other side, Thelma was grinning, nudging her with a sharp elbow.

Stirring, she picked up her knife and put a dab of butter on her bread. Frances couldn't believe what he'd just said. Was that, in his strange way of talking, a declaration of love? A hint at a future together? Frances wanted that...she did. She didn't want to be without Cecil either, but one thing kept worrying her mind. Spending a lifetime with his mother always making remarks about her. It was obvious she and Cecil were developing into more than friendship, but how would his mother react?

As soon as she wondered that, she felt a wave of worry wash over her. There was more to be concerned about than how his mother felt about her. War loomed on the horizon. Surely, his mother felt the strain as well. She might be sending her children off, maybe never to see them again. Frances wasn't a mother yet, obviously, but she couldn't imagine how terrifying that would be.

She glanced over at him. He was listening to a story another fellow was telling, and laughing. It was good to see him laugh, to see him happy. In that moment, Frances realized, that's all she wanted. The happiness of those she loved.

The question was, would she get it?

Chapter 9

After Thelma quietly slipped out of the room to leave for the factory, Frances yawned and sat up. She got ready for work, boiling herself water for a cup of tea, slicing off a bit of bread and covering it with jam, and getting dressed. Outside, it looked to be a perfect day. The kind that held such promise of something good happening.

As she waited for the bus, birds landed on the tree overhead, chirping and tweeting. It seemed even nature was content. The last few months had been going well. As the world had moved into 1941, threats of war grew bolder, but so far, none of the men had been called into a draft. Rations also weren't required, so there was a slightly more relaxed feeling. It wasn't too difficult to find what you wanted at the store, and life...well, life didn't really seem too different from before the president signed the peacetime draft.

Frances was still concerned, though she and Cecil didn't talk much about the war. Instead, they talked about themselves: the things they liked, what they hoped for, and their families. Their spare moments, which weren't many, were spent together. Sometimes they got ice cream, other times picnicked at a park, and occasionally went to a movie. Cecil was anxious to see the new, talking version of *The Mark of Zorro* when it came out in November.

She'd been invited several more times to dinner with Cecil's family and had enjoyed meeting his two younger brothers. Recently, it almost seemed as though Cecil's mother might be softening toward her slightly. Last night, she'd offered to help with the dishes after the meal, and this time was taken up on the offer. She and Mrs. Hall hadn't talked much, but it was almost a companionable silence, she thought to herself as the bus bumped over the road toward the factory and her morning shift.

The drive back had been nice. Instead of letting her out in front of the boarding house, Cecil had pulled around the side. There was enough light Frances could see he was digging for something in his jacket pocket. Curiously, she looked to see what it was.

After a moment, he pulled out a small box. "Here," he said, thrusting it at her.

Frances took it, untied a white ribbon, and lifted the lid. When she looked inside, she gasped. There was a small silver bracelet with a heart on it. "It's beautiful," she told him.

"Engraved it," he told her.

She turned it over. "Cecil loves Frances," she read. Her eyes filled with tears, and she leaned forward, hugging him tightly. "It's wonderful. I love it, and I'll keep it forever," she told him.

Cecil ducked his head and grinned. "Walk you in?" he asked.

She nodded, and they'd gone inside. Thelma had made a fuss over the bracelet, and Frances hoped one day her sister had a beau too. She deserved someone to make her as happy as Frances felt.

The bus pulled up and dropped her off, and Frances hurried into the building. As much as she had wanted to wear the bracelet today, she knew it was a hazard, but it was tucked carefully inside of a small jewelry box she had in her room.

Clocking in at work, Frances took her usual spot. Several women rushed in at the last moment with puffy eyes and tear-stained cheeks. She was curious, but there wasn't a chance to check on them. The work was too demanding, both physically and mentally.

During her short break, she normally ate a few bites of a packed meal and closed her eyes to rest, much like the other women did. But today, several of them were clustered, whispering.

"What's wrong?" Frances asked, concerned. "Can I help in some way?"

"No one can," Betty, who'd been there the longest, hiccupped. "My boyfriend was called up in the draft."

"Mine too," Mary Ellen sniffed.

Frances felt a strange feeling in her stomach. What of Cecil? While she'd not heard anything from him, surely he would have told her if that was the case. She gave the girls hugs. "Being called up doesn't mean you won't see them again," she soothed. "It just means that you have the most incredible, selfless boyfriends. Going off to serve their country in a time of need."

The whistle sounded, signaling the break was over.

It was all Frances could do to keep her mind on her work. As soon as her shift was over, she rushed to the bus stop and waited impatiently for the bus. A restless feeling grew within her. If men were being called up, how many? Would Cecil be? Is this why she had that feeling that something wasn't right?

When the bus let her off, she walked as quickly as she could without looking rushed to the hamburger stand. There were no customers at the moment. She waved to Jimmy, and asked, "Cecil there?"

He nodded. "Cecil! Your girl is here!"

Cecil's head popped up through the kitchen window opening. "Hallo!" he called.

"Hallo!" she answered with a grin.

"Everything alright?" Cecil asked, scrunching his face.

"Yes," Frances answered. She started to explain her strange feeling, but stopped. It would make her feel silly. Nothing was wrong. *I'm such a worrywart. I'm not going to bother him.* Frances shrugged, "I just wanted to see you a moment. That's all."

"Wait there," Cecil said. He disappeared, then came to the front counter. "Coke?" he asked.

"I better not. Thelma will worry if I'm not back soon," she said, a little reluctantly.

He nodded. "I'm glad you stopped by," he said. He reached across and squeezed her hand. "Looking forward to our date Saturday."

"Me too," Frances agreed. She stepped back and gave a little wave. "See you soon."

He waved in return, then headed back to the kitchen. Feeling better, Frances turned toward the boarding house. Thelma looked up as soon as she came in. "I wondered where you were," her sister said. "Was the bus late?"

"No," Frances said, pulling off her hat and shoes. "Two of the girls at work were upset today. Their boyfriends were called up in the draft."

Thelma nodded. "A few on my shift were crying. It seems some of the men are also enlisting before they get called."

"Well," Frances continued, "I just felt so nervous all of a sudden. Doesn't that sound silly? But I wanted to see Cecil. I just...had this feeling. When the bus dropped me off, I went over there a moment to see if he was there. I just got back from the stand."

Thelma nodded. "I understand. Was...was he called up?"

"He seemed okay. He didn't say anything and I'm sure he would have told me."

"I think so too," Thelma said. She stood. "I'm going to go down to the sitting room a little."

"I'll join you," Frances said. "For some reason, I've still got this restless feeling I can't explain. And it's so odd, because this morning everything felt fine. Perfect, even."

"That happens sometimes," Thelma said.

She led the way, and Frances followed with her book. They joined a few others in the sitting room. Thelma was quietly talking to someone near the window. Frances soon lost herself in the book, only looking up when she heard a familiar voice.

"If he's not here, do you know where my Cecil works?"

"Mrs. Hall?"

The older woman stood in the doorway of the boarding house. She looked like she'd been crying. Her hands were wringing her purse, and when she saw Frances, she nearly burst in, rushing up to her and grabbing her hands. "Frances! How do I get to Cecil's work?"

Taken aback, Frances stammered, "Why, it's not too far away. I'll tell you if you like."

Mrs. Hall shook her head. "Can you just take me? I'm worried I'd never find it. I got so turned around getting here from the bus."

"Of course," she answered. "Let me just get my purse and walking shoes."

Hurriedly Frances went to her room and returned a moment later. Thelema was standing next to Mrs. Hall, keeping her company. They both looked up as she returned. Thelma's face looked grim. "Is...everything okay?" Frances asked.

Mrs. Hall let out a sob as an answer, and held her handkerchief to her face. She shook her head and a sick lump formed in Frances's stomach.

"This way," Frances said, setting off down the sidewalk. "He's not too far away. I don't think it will be crowded this time of day. He ought to be able to talk."

The other woman nodded, and they walked silently.

"Right there," Frances pointed. "I'll take you up to it."

"You are a good girl," Mrs. Hall said. She stopped suddenly. "Frances, forgive an old, selfish woman, won't you?" Her eyes were filled with sadness. "Really...you are a very sweet girl, and my Cecil couldn't do any better choosing you."

Frances just shook her head, smiled, and reached out to pat Mrs. Hall's hand. "There's nothing to forgive. Now, let me get you to him."

As they approached the hamburger stand, Frances was relieved to see there were no customers.

"Back again?" Jimmy asked.

"Sure am. Say, this is Cecil's mother. She's come a long way, and needs to speak with him. Can you get him?"

"Sure." Jimmy disappeared.

"I'll wait over here to give you privacy, but that way I can help you get back to the bus stop," Frances said, moving to a stool.

Mrs. Hall nodded. "Thank you."

Cecil came around the corner. "Ma?"

"Oh, Cecil!" Mrs. Hall nearly threw herself at him. "You got this in the mail." She stepped back to open her purse and remove an envelope.

At the far side of the hamburger stand, Frances and Jimmy were pretending as hard as they could not to be watching. Jimmy was wiping the counter as slowly as he could, and Frances was sipping at a glass of water he'd given her. Their eyes met. Jimmy's were filled with worry. Frances was sure hers were the same. She swallowed hard against the bitter taste in her mouth.

Mrs. Hall burst into tears again, and Frances glanced over. Cecil had put his hands in his pockets, slouching a little. "Ma," he said. "It's what has to be done. I'll be fine." He looked up and met Frances's eyes.

Hers filled with tears. "Cecil?" she asked, her voice watery. There was no point in pretending not to listen. "Is...everything okay?"

He walked over, held out the letter with a grim expression, and said, "My draft number was chosen."

Chapter 10

Frances sucked in a deep breath. Everything seemed to spin, and she felt dizzy. Cecil grabbed her elbow and helped her to sit on a nearby stool. Mrs. Hall joined her. Frances couldn't tear her eyes off the letter. *Called up for the draft.* Her Cecil. No wonder his mother was so upset. She was too.

The words she'd said earlier to the girls at the factory came to mind and felt hollow. Why had she said them? To make the others feel better, of course, but war was filled with so much uncertainty. Yes, there was a certain pride to be had, knowing one's loved one was serving and fighting, protecting the home front. But...there was also so much worry.

Her lower lip trembled, and she finally looked at him. Cecil had shoved his hands in his pockets and was slouching. She'd learned this was his behavior when he didn't quite know what to do. He was looking at his shoes.

Frances looked at Mrs. Hall, who looked incredibly distraught. Behind them, Jimmy was still wiping, but his rag wasn't on the counter, instead it hovered above the counter as he stared.

It was up to her to bring a change to the sudden mood of despair.

But how?

Sucking in a deep breath, Frances put on a smile and straightened her shoulders. "Well then," she said. "Mrs. Hall, I suspect you and I had best get to work. We're going to need to make sure Cecil has enough whatever it is that he will need. We don't know where he will be sent, but some nice socks, gloves, and scarves made with love never hurt anybody."

She pushed herself off the stool and rested her hand on Cecil's arm. "We've kept you long enough. I know the dinner rush will start soon and you've got to cook. I'll help your mother get back to the bus stop, and see the driver looks after her. We'll chat on the way, and find out what everyone else is doing for their men as they are sent to training."

Cecil had looked up and was giving her a grateful look. "Swell, swell," he said. He helped his mother stand and kissed her cheek. "I'll stop by Sunday, Ma."

"Bring Frances with you," his mother said, as she moved toward the sidewalk. "I'll make a roast."

He nodded, and waved, then vanished into the hamburger stand. Frances looked over her shoulder to see Jimmy had vanished too. No doubt to check on his friend.

"This way," Frances said softly.

Mrs. Hall followed her. "Knitting is a good idea," she said. "Is there a good place to buy yarn here?"

"I'll show you my favorite store," Frances offered. "It's down this street."

The two went a few blocks, not saying much. Frances was lost in her own thoughts and worries, and no doubt Cecil's mother was the same. When they got to the shop, the bell above the door tinkled as they entered. Frances led the way to the back, where cubbies and baskets of yarn stood. Mrs. Hall stared at each skein with a critical eye.

"Help you find something, ladies?" a man asked.

"Yes," Mrs. Hall said, her voice wobbling. "My boy..." she stopped.

"He's been called for the draft," Frances continued, her voice low. "We are going to knit for him."

"I've got just what you'll need over here," the clerk said. "Moved it to the front yesterday. All the approved colors and materials."

They followed him, and both Frances and Mrs. Hall selected several skeins. After purchasing it, they went back outside.

"I'm better at scarves and gloves," Mrs. Hall said. "How are you at socks?"

"Not too bad," Frances said. "My sister is really good. I'll have her help me if it gets tricky."

Mrs. Hall nodded and strode along the sidewalk toward the bus stop. In the distance, they saw it approach, and she turned to Frances. "Thank you," she said, and as the bus came to a stop, she climbed on and took a seat.

Frances stuck her head in the door. "Please help her get where she needs to go," she said.

The driver waved and the bus left. Frances watched until it was out of sight, and then the emotions she'd been holding in threatened to explode. She turned and hurried back to the boarding house.

Later. There will be time for tears later.

She went in, and Thelma approached her anxiously. Without saying a word, she wrapped her arms around Frances. Frances held her sister and felt a sob trying to escape.

"There, there, dear," her sister said. "I've water warmed for some tea. Come, let's sit." Thelma kept her arm around Frances and led her to their room.

Frances drew in a shaky breath. "His number was called," she said.

"I figured as much," Thelma said, fussing over the hot water and tea. Offering a cup to Frances, she took hers and sat on her bed. Frances took the chair. "There's a lot of uncertainty right now."

"There is," Frances agreed. "One thing I do know, is that if he asked me to, I'll wait for him." She drank deeply of the tea. "This is good. Thank you."

"What if he doesn't?" Thelma asked. "What if he wants you to marry him, and follow him to training?"

Frances blinked a few times. "I...I don't know. We've not really talked about that."

"Well, you better think about it," Thelma warned. "A lot of fellas are getting married right now. That way if something happens to them, their sweethearts get any possible benefits. Some are also wanting to start a family without delay."

"That always happens, wartime," Frances murmured. She looked into her tea for a moment before meeting her sister's eyes. "I'm not sure what I'll say. But he's not even asked yet, so there's no use my thinking about it."

Thelma nodded and drank from her cup. "Time for dinner," she said. "Let's go."

Frances watched her sister leave before pushing herself out of the chair. She wasn't hungry, and Thelma had given her a lot to think on. If Cecil did ask her to marry, what would she say? Perhaps he wouldn't, and he'd just want her to wait for him. As she closed the door behind her, another thought sprang to mind. If she did marry, would Thelma be okay? They each paid half the rent...the entire room would be very hard to cover on a single salary. Though her sister hadn't brought that up, it's possible she was thinking it.

All of a sudden Frances felt very selfish. It didn't matter what happened, one person might be left hurt. Thelma and Cecil were the most important people in her life. How could she do that to either of them?

Chapter 11

At work, Frances joined the other girls talking about the draft. They agreed to get together and have a knitting party, to send their men off with whatever they might need that they could provide.

"I'm getting married next week," Sally said suddenly.

"Why?" Frances asked. "That's so sudden! How will you plan?"

"We aren't doing much," Sally said. "My mother's baking the cake and doing a meal. My grandmother is helping her. It will just be simple, in the living room. I don't have time to get a new dress, but Mother is asking a neighbor to alter her wedding gown for me to wear."

"I'm sure it will be lovely, even if it's simple," Frances said.

"What about you?" Sally asked. "I know you and Cecil are fairly serious. Has he asked you to marry him?"

She shook her head. "No, not yet."

Sally pressed, "If he does, will you?"

Frances was quiet. "I'm not sure."

Nodding, Sally said, "Let me have your address. When Johnny and I get married, we're going to drive down to where he reports for basic training and live there. This is my last week at the factory."

"I hadn't thought about that part, either," Frances confessed. "Moving away, to be with someone at basic training."

"Not everyone is," Mary said from across the room. "I'm not. I've got to keep working. Where Frank is reporting, there isn't much housing. I'll live here still, with my mother, and wait for him to come back."

Frances was glad when the whistle blew and everyone returned to their shifts. She didn't want to hear anymore. As the machinery hummed and thumped in the background, so did her thoughts, though she kept trying to keep them away.

What would she do if Cecil asked? Did she want him to ask? It was a large step, getting married, and an even larger one to get married before a war. Add in the fact he'd be off in basic training, her life would suddenly and drastically change, and she'd be leaving Thelma...and how would Thelma manage?

By the end of the day, her temples and eyes ached with worry, and on the bus she rested her head against the cool glass pane. How was it that all at once everything had become so complicated?

The bus pulled up to her stop, and she gathered her handbag and rose. To her surprise, Cecil was there, waiting for her.

"Why are you here?" she asked. "I thought you'd be at work."

"I am," he said, hands shoved in his pockets. "I asked for a few minutes so I could run over and see you off the bus."

Frances smiled and stood next to him. "Walk you back?" she asked.

He grinned at her. "I'd like that. Stay for a Coke?"

She nodded. "I'd like that," she said quietly.

The air seemed to crackle with something she couldn't quite explain. There was this feeling that Cecil wanted to say something, but he wasn't talking. They walked a few steps more, when he suddenly reached out, grabbing her arm and stopping her. "Frances," he said.

Her eyes met his. "What's wrong?" she asked, concerned. "Has something happened?"

She wasn't sure she could handle the stress of anything else. Worry grew in her stomach, spreading its way through her chest, arms, and legs. She felt heavy and tingly and tight.

"I want to ask you something," he said. "I found out where I'll be sent."

"Where?"

"San Francisco."

Frances gasped. "So far? All the way to California?"

He nodded. "Yep. Pretty far away. I hear it's pretty. Different from here. It...could be a fresh start."

She nodded slowly. "I see."

Was this Cecil's way of telling her goodbye? That he wanted a fresh start? Her lower lip trembled. Of course. It made sense. For someone to get married or to keep a sweetheart right before leaving for training, knowing they may be sent to war was a terrible thing, really. You missed that person. It might even be distracting. Just like in her job, distractions could prove dangerous, and in the case of training and war, deadly.

Frances lifted her chin, refusing to let her tears fall. "I...I'm sure that you'll quickly adjust. The...the weather, I hear, is quite nice."

"Yep." He dug his hands so far into his pockets and slouched so deeply, she wondered if she should stoop, as she was suddenly much taller than him.

"Look," Cecil suddenly straightened, and reached for her arm again. "I'm not very good with this kind of thing. But...I guess." He looked away for a moment, then back at her. "It'll be different. It might be nice. But it'll be lonely without you. I guess what I'm asking is will you go with me?"

Frances looked at him, feeling a little confused. Cecil caught the expression and clarified, "As my wife. Will you marry me, and we'll move there together? Start our life together? They've got some big department stores out there. I know you always wanted to work in one of those."

His eyes were nearly burning into her. Frances felt her heart start to thud. There it was...the question she'd both longed for and dreaded. How...how would she answer?

How *should* she answer?

Her legs felt weak, and she turned her head, looking for something to lean again. Behind her was a short wall. With wobbly legs she went to it and sat.

Cecil appeared, and in his hand was a small box. He opened the lid. "Will you, Frances?" he repeated. "Will you marry me?" He looked down briefly, then back up. "I understand it's a long way away. From your folks, your sister. You'd be giving up your job, and everyone and everything you know. I promise, we'll come back one day. I just...I don't know when."

Frances could hardly form thoughts, let alone words, but as she looked at him, she remembered something he'd told her, and suddenly everything made sense. She smiled and whispered, "Where you go, I go."

Raising his head, Cecil's eyes were filled with hope. "Does that mean yes?"

She nodded. "It means yes, Cecil. Yes, forever."

Cecil slid the ring onto her hand, and then kissed her. Frances blushed, grateful no one was passing by to see them, but she reluctantly stepped back as he released her. "I better go. Might be someone needing a hamburger."

"I'd love that Coke still," she said.

He took her hand and they walked to the hamburger stand. Jimmy was wiping the counter down and grinned when he saw them. The small radio behind the counter started to play, and Irving Berlin's voice trickled out, playing "How Deep is the Ocean".

"Couple of Cokes, Jimmy," Cecil said. "For me, and my future misses."

Epilogue

Frances tearfully hugged Thelma while Cecil loaded her suitcases in the car. True to his word, once the bullet holes were patched, and the truck was painted, it looked good as new. No one would be gawking at them as they drove out to San Francisco. The hidden compartments, originally intended for moonshine, were actually quite handy at holding some of their belongings.

It had been a whirlwind last two weeks. They'd had a civil wedding, she'd told her parents goodbye, and Cecil had promised that once she got a new job, she could keep setting aside a little to help her folks buy a house. That warmed her heart.

"Drive safely," Thelma said, wiping her eyes.

"Are you sure you'll be fine without me?" Frances asked anxiously.

"Of course!" Thelma said. "I'm moving in with a girl from the factory. We'll go halves on the rent, same as you and I did. The room is even a little bigger, so that's nice." She lowered her voice, "I understand she knows quite a few fellas, and so I'm hoping to meet one myself."

Frances laughed and embraced her sister again. "I'll write," she promised.

"Picture postcards," Thelma ordered. "I want to see where you go."

She nodded. "I will. I'll send them to Mama and Papa too."

They stood looking at each other. "I...I guess this is goodbye," Frances said, her throat feeling tight.

Cecil came up behind her. "Not goodbye," he said, looking around, his head turning slowly to take in the boarding house, the street, and the places they'd made memories together. "Not goodbye at all. It's see you soon. We'll be back, but when we are, it'll be in our own house, and with our own family."

Thelma smiled, and the three of them looked at each other for a long moment. Finally, she broke the silence,

"Get going, you two! Cecil, next time I see you, you'll need to grill us some hamburgers. No one makes one finer than you."

Cecil grinned, ducked his head, and jammed his hands in his pockets. "Will do," he promised. He opened the door for Frances and waited as the sisters hugged once more.

"Wait, before I go." Sniffling a little, Frances pressed a small package into Thelma's hand.

"What this?" Thelma asked, untying the string around the brown paper. Frances didn't answer, but as the brown wrapping fell away, Thelma gasped, and more tears fell from her eyes. She held the bar of lavender soap, wrapped in purple paper and tied up in a tiny purple ribbon, to her nose and breathed in deeply. "You shouldn't have," she said, and embraced Frances tightly.

Suddenly, with a scowl, she pulled back. "You didn't get it from that old Mrs. Dixon, did you?"

"I'd never," Frances swore, holding up a hand. "Cecil and I found it when we went on a drive."

"Good." Thelma breathed in the scent once more and smiled.

There was no more delaying it. With a long look and a nod, Frances and Thelma gave one last embrace and Frances slid into the seat of the truck.

The window was already down, and she called goodbye and waved as they drove off until she could no longer see her sister or the boarding house. She looked down at her finger, where a new ring sat. A wedding ring. Her heart felt heavy. It was a mixture of happiness and sorrow. Inside was a little excitement too. She'd never been so far, and she was looking forward to the adventure, even if it might be a little scary.

"You ready?" Cecil asked. "It's a long drive."

Frances smiled at him. "Where you go, I go."

"Funny thing that," Cecil said, steering onto the highway.

She turned to him. "How so?"

Cecil reached over and took her hand. "I was about to say the same thing."

Thank you for taking the time to read Frances!

Could I ask for one small favor? Reviews like yours on Amazon mean so much to me and help others to find my books! Even just a single line means a lot!

Stop by my website to see everything I've written and keep up to date! Join my newsletter for exclusive sneak peeks and surprises.

www.sarahlambbooks.com

About the Author

Sarah Lamb is the mother of two boys and wife to a teacher. She spends her days writing and editing books in the beautiful Shenandoah Valley.

She also writes non-fiction books, with an emphasis on self-advocacy and food allergy awareness, as well as books for middle grade and young adult readers.

Want more of Sarah's books? She writes for children and adults! Find them all on Amazon. Here are just a few.

Fiction for Adults

Caroline (Runaway Brides of the West Series)
The Christmas Treasure (Holiday Cottage Series)
Mathilda (Rescue Me: Mail-Order Brides Series)
Louise (Rescue Me: Mail-Order Brides Series)
Frances (Women of the Blue Ridge Series)
Second Chance in Pumpkin City (Pumpkin City Series)
A Gunslinger for Grace (Mail-Order Papa Series)
An Angel for Alice (A Christmas Eve short story)
A Second Chance for Beatrice (A Christmas Eve short story)